The Little Match Girl

Written by Hans Christian Andersen

(retold by Carrie Weston)

Illustrated by Fabian Negrin

It was a cold and snowy New Year's Eve. The wind howled through the bare trees and blew snowflakes down the street.

From inside the town houses came the merry sound of laughter and singing. Crackling fires in the hearth gave a soft light at the windows. The smell of roasting dinners filled the air as families prepared to celebrate the end of the old year and the start of a new one.

Outside the street was empty. All except for one young girl wearing a thin dress with a shawl pulled fast around her. She shivered in the cold, rubbed her frozen fingers and tightly clutched a tiny bundle in her hands.

Suddenly, out of the gloom raced a carriage pulled by two fine black horses. The girl hurried out of its way as fast as she could, for she was sure the driver would not see her in the dark. It was hard to run; her toes were numb with cold and she wore only rags around her feet.

As the carriage thundered past, the girl fell to the ground and dropped her little bundle in the snow. Out spilled the matches onto the pavement.

"Oh!" she sobbed desperately, "I must find every last one!" Her fingers searched in the crisp snow until she had picked up each and every match that had fallen. With shaking hands she tried hopelessly to tie them back into a bundle.

Eventually, she sat back on the pavement, buried her face
in her hands and sobbed until her whole body shook.

"Father will be so angry!" she cried to herself. "I haven't
sold one bundle of matches all day. Not one!"

Snowflakes swirled through the night air and settled on
the little match girl's hair.

"I have not a ha'penny, not even a farthing to take home,"
she lamented.

Just then, she heard the chuckle of a baby coming from a house nearby. The delicious smell of baking cut through the night air and the warm glow from the window seemed to draw her closer.

The girl pulled her shawl around her shoulders and painfully shuffled nearer to the light. She rubbed the frost from the pane and pressed her face longingly to the glass.

She could just make out a large room where a family sat around a table talking and laughing. A baby boy bounced on his mother's knee whilst his brothers and sisters tucked into a fine feast of goose and plates of steaming vegetables.

The match girl was convinced she could smell the delicious food even from outside in the cold.

In the corner of the room she could see a Christmas tree,
glowing with a hundred tiny candles.

The little match seller shivered and hung her head sadly as she recalled her own cold, dark lodgings.

She thought of the leaky roof and the rags that hung at the windows. She thought of the empty fireplace and the bare table. She remembered how her father would bang his fists and shout every time she displeased him.

Then the image of her grandmother came into her mind, the only person who had ever showed her love and kindness.

The little match girl turned away from the window with tears rolling down her cheeks and hobbled along the dark street. How her poor, frozen feet hurt; how stiff and cold her fingers were.

Soon the wretched child in the thin, ragged dress could go no further. She huddled in an empty doorway where she found some shelter from the bitter wind.

In the night sky above, a shooting star plunged towards the Earth.

"When a star falls, a new angel is born," she whispered to herself through chattering teeth, for that was the story her beloved grandmother had told her.

The harsh wind howled, the snow swirled and the girl
longed to light just one match to feel the flame near her icy
fingers.

"How wasteful!" her father would shout, but a terrible
chill was gripping her heart. With trembling fingers, she
struck a match.

SSSSCRITCH!

The match burnt brightly as it flickered and spluttered in her hands. Her eyes shone briefly in the golden light.

But all too soon the flame died out and the night seemed colder and lonelier than ever before.

As fast as she was able, the little girl fumbled for another match and struck it.

SSSSCRITCH!

The flame burst into life. This time, she cupped her hand carefully over the tiny fire and, as she did so, it seemed to the little match girl that she was basking in the glow of a burning stove, warming her frozen hands and feet…

The match went out and the stove disappeared.

Before she could stop herself, the poor child lit another match. This time, she found herself at the window of the house again.

Now she seemed to pass through the glass and found herself inside, seated by the roaring fire. In the glow of the match light the girl saw the children beckon her to join the feast.

She sat at the end of the great table, with the warmth of the fire on her back. She took a plate piled high with juicy meats and steaming roast potatoes ...

The match burned out and the food vanished.

She lit another match, and another.

She was standing by the Christmas tree, wearing a silk gown and comfortable slippers and she felt great warmth and happiness. Another match and there, in the firelight, stood her grandmother, smiling, her arms open wide to greet her. "Grandmother!" called out the little girl as the match burned away.

Her fingers shook violently as she lit match after match, desperate to keep her grandmother's face before her.

"Please don't go!" she cried out. "Stay with me!"

Soon the flame from the last match died out, but this time grandmother did not disappear. She took the little girl in her arms, kissed her golden hair and hugged her tightly.

In the cold dawn of New Year's Day a child lay in a
doorway. Her eyes were shut and her hair hung lifeless
around her pale cheeks, but her lips were frozen in the most
beautiful smile.

The ground by her feet was littered with black, spent
matchsticks.

"Poor little thing!" cried the townspeople when they found
her body. "She was just trying to keep herself warm!"

The little match girl could no longer hear them.
She was far, far away, beyond hunger or cold, with
someone who loved her best of all.

Hans Christian Andersen (1805 – 1875)

Hans Christian Anderson is one of the world's best-loved children's writers. He was born in Denmark in April 1805, and his birthday is still celebrated there today.

Hans Christian Andersen had a very poor and unhappy childhood. He made use of his experience when he wrote his many fairy tales for children.

His father earned a living as a shoemaker and read to young Hans every day. However, when Hans was 11 years old, his father died and the family became very poor indeed. His mother washed clothes to earn a little extra money but Hans did not have the chance to go to school. He grew up in poverty and often suffered from neglect as his mother had very little time to spend with him.

When he was 14 years old, Hans ran away to Copenhagen, the capital city of Denmark, and began to write stories.

In his fairy stories, Hans Christian Andersen explored people's feelings and the way they behave towards each other. The messages in his tales were very popular in Victorian Britain.

Many of Andersen's stories are about different ways of being happy, or how a bad beginning can lead to a happy end.

Hans Christian Andersen wanted to give children hope and joy, and his stories are still told in many different languages all around the world.

You may have read, seen or heard some of Hans Christian Andersen's fairy stories, such as; *The Ugly Duckling, The Emperor's New Clothes, The Little Mermaid, Thumbelina, The Snow Queen, The Princess and the Pea, The Ice Maiden* and *The Red Shoes.*